Find
Anthony
Ant

This edition published in Great Britain in 2006
by Boxer Books Limited.
www.boxerbooks.com

First published in Great Britain in 1993
by Orion Children's Books, under the title
Amazing Anthony Ant.

Hardback ISBN 1-905417-05-5
Paperback ISBN 1-905417-06-3

Printed in China

For Ann,
David and Nicola

Are you an amazing Anthony Ant
finder? If so, can you find the odd
one out among all the Anthony Ants
on the endpapers of this book?

Find
Anthony Ant

Lorna and Graham Philpot

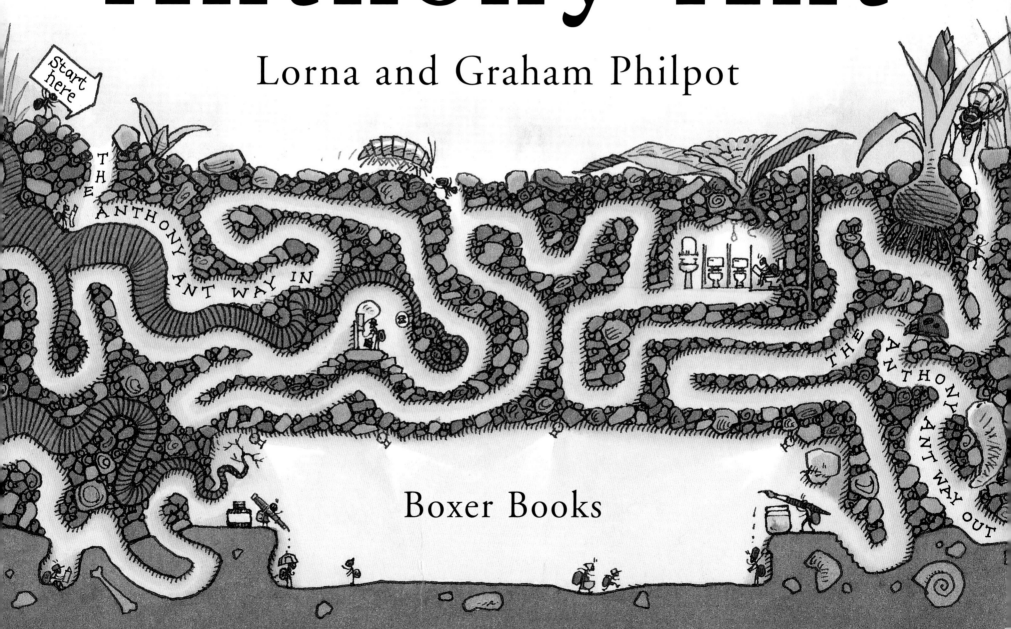

Boxer Books

1

The ants came marching **one by one.** Anthony stopped...

WAY IN

BEETLE LANE

Grub Shop

PLUM TREE TRUNK ROAD

or or

To eat
a plum?

To buy
bubblegum?

To beat
a drum?

Find Anthony Ant.

2

The ants came marching
two by two.
Anthony stopped...

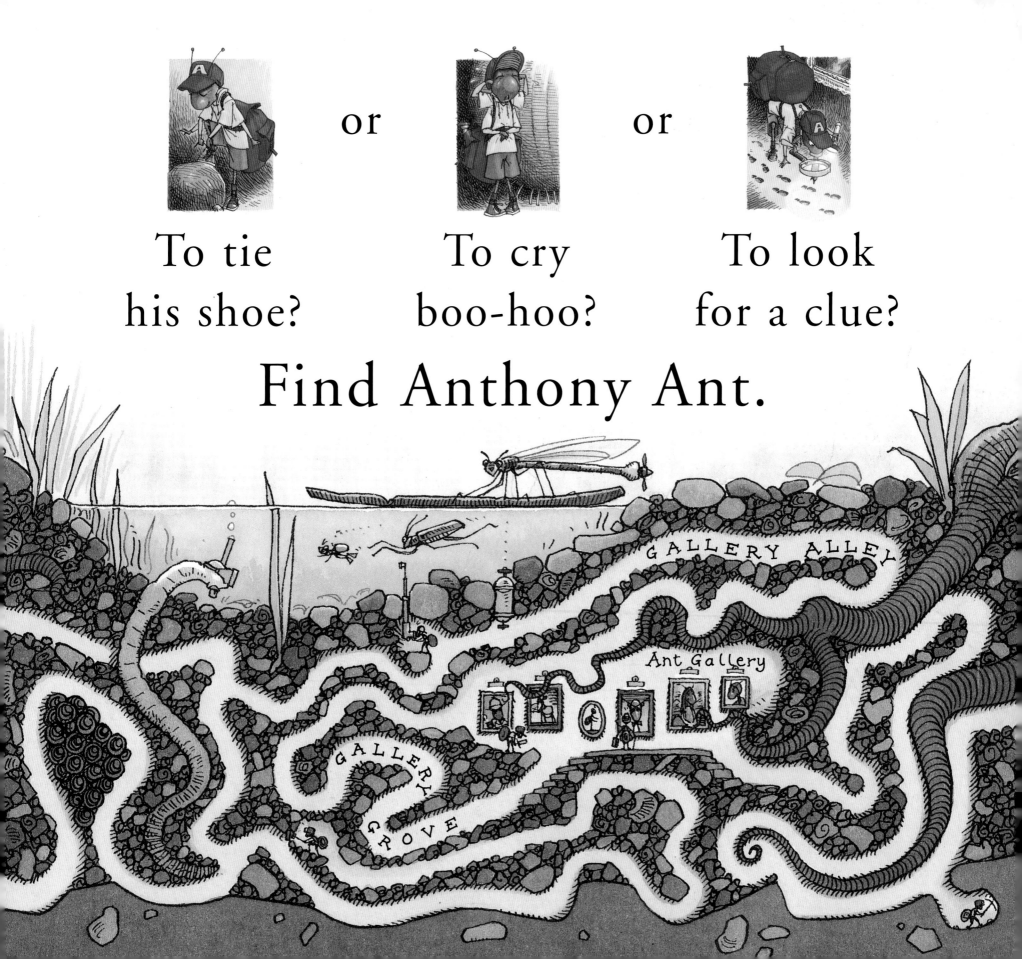

or

or

To tie
his shoe?

To cry
boo-hoo?

To look
for a clue?

Find Anthony Ant.

GALLERY ALLEY

Ant Gallery

GALLERY
GROVE

3

The ants came marching **three by three.**
Anthony stopped...

WOODWORM WAY

PINE TREE ROUTE

ANT ATTIC

ANTEA HOUSE

BUG BASEMENT

 or  or

To climb
a tree?

To watch
TV?

Because he's
hurt his knee?

Find Anthony Ant.

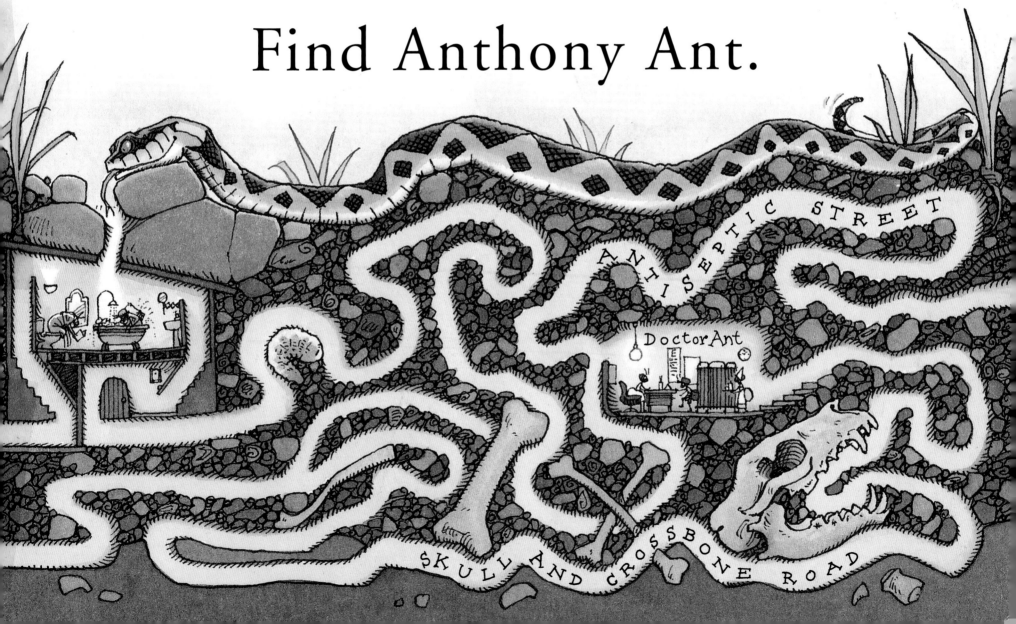

4 The ants came marching
four by four.
Anthony stopped...

 or  or

To knock on
the door?

To ask
for more?

To sweep
the floor?

Find Anthony Ant.

5

The ants came marching
five by five.
Anthony stopped....

To visit
a hive?

or

To jiggle
and jive?

or

To go for
a drive?

Find Anthony Ant.

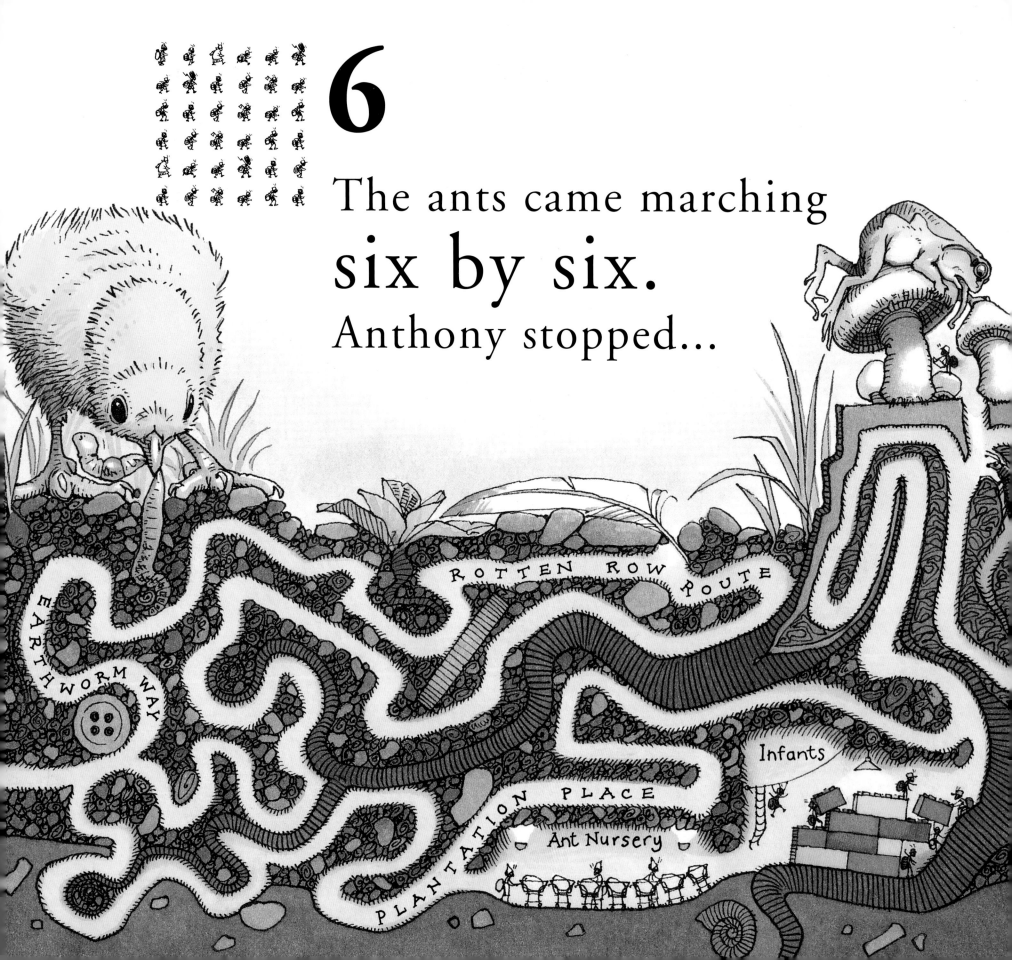

6

The ants came marching
six by six.
Anthony stopped...

To tickle
the chicks?

or

To stack
the bricks?

or

The Great
Anthony

To perform
magic tricks?

Find Anthony Ant.

7

The ants came marching **seven by seven.** Anthony stopped...

To chat with Kevin?

or

To hide in a cavern?

or

To count to eleven?

Find Anthony Ant.

8

The ants came marching
eight by eight.
Anthony stopped...

 or  or

To lick
his plate?

To look
for a gate?

To check
his weight?

Find Anthony Ant.

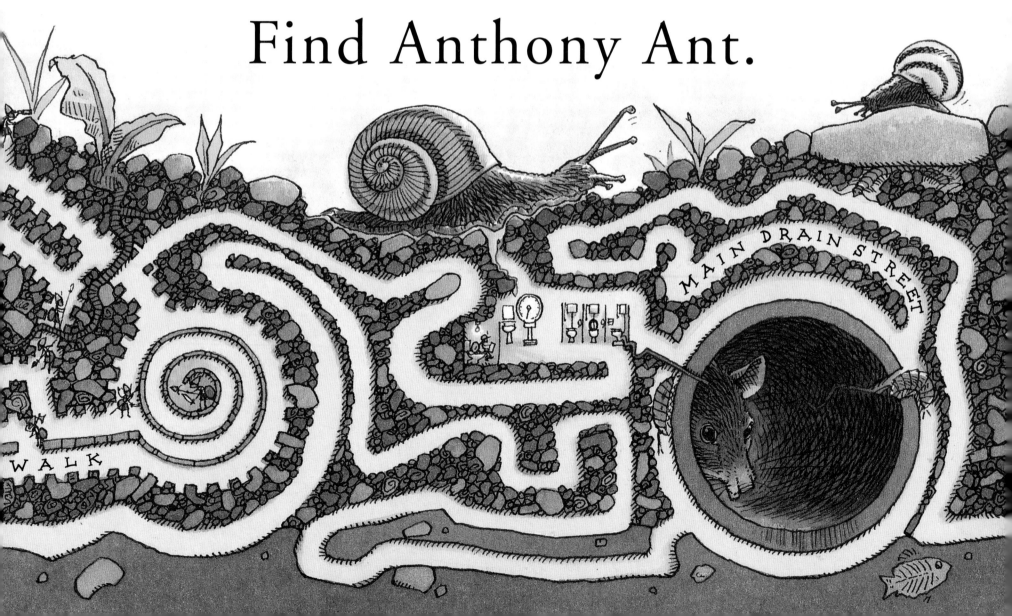

9

The ants came marching
nine by nine.
Anthony stopped...

 or  or

To hang socks on the line? To read a sign? To shout, "That hat's mine"?

Find Anthony Ant.

10

The ants came marching
ten by ten.
Anthony stopped...

or

or

To feed
the hen?

To write
with a pen?

To read
it again?

Find Anthony Ant.

Did you find me?